Selected Poems

Selected Poems

RICHARD MURPHY

FABER AND FABER
London & Boston

First published in 1979
by Faber and Faber Limited
3 Queen Square London WC1
Printed in Great Britain by
Latimer Trend & Company Ltd Plymouth
All rights reserved

© Richard Murphy, 1979

British Library Cataloguing in Publication Data

Murphy, Richard
Selected poems of Richard Murphy.
821'.9'14   PR6025.U6973A17

ISBN 0-571-11357-5

To my Mother

Acknowledgments

Some of these poems have appeared in *American Review*, *Encounter*, *Hibernia*, *The Irish Times*, *Irish University Review*, *Listen*, *The Listener*, *London Magazine*, *Massachusetts Review*, *New Irish Writing* in *The Irish Press*, the *New Review*, *The New Statesman*, the *New York Review of Books*, *Poetry* (Chicago), *Sewanee Review* and *The Times Literary Supplement*. Some of the poems have been revised for this edition.

Acknowledgments are made also to the Arts Council of Great Britain for awards in 1967 and 1975; to the BBC and RTE and the Australian Broadcasting Corporation for having broadcast some of these poems on radio and television.

Contents

Sailing to an Island

The boom above my knees lifts, and the boat
Drops, and the surge departs, departs, my cheek
Kissed and rejected, kissed, as the gaff sways
A tangent, cuts the infinite sky to red
Maps, and the mast draws eight and eight across
Measureless blue, the boatmen sing or sleep.

We point all day for our chosen island,
Clare, with its crags purpled by legend:
There under castles the hot O'Malleys,
Daughters of Granuaile, the pirate queen
Who boarded a Turk with a blunderbuss,
Comb red hair and assemble cattle.
Across the shelved Atlantic groundswell
Plumbed by the sun's kingfisher rod,
We sail to locate in sea, earth and stone
The myth of a shrewd and brutal swordswoman
Who piously endowed an abbey.
Seven hours we try against wind and tide,
Tack and return, making no headway.
The north wind sticks like a gag in our teeth.

Encased in a mirage, steam on the water,
Loosely we coast where hideous rocks jag,
An acropolis of cormorants, an extinct
Volcano where spiders spin, a purgatory
Guarded by hags and bristled with breakers.

The breeze as we plunge slowly stiffens:
There are hills of sea between us and land,
Between our hopes and the island harbour.

A child vomits. The boat veers and bucks.
There is no refuge on the gannet's cliff.
We are far, far out: the hull is rotten,
The spars are splitting, the rigging is frayed,
And our helmsman laughs uncautiously.
What of those who must earn their living
On the ribald face of a mad mistress?
We in holiday fashion know
This is the boat that belched its crew
Dead on the shingle in the Cleggan disaster.

Now she dips, and the sail hits the water.
She luffs to a squall; is struck; and shudders.
Someone is shouting. The boom, weak as scissors,
Has snapped. The boatman is praying.
Orders thunder and canvas cannonades.
She smothers in spray. We still have a mast;
The oar makes a boom. I am told to cut
Cords out of fishing-lines, fasten the jib.
Ropes lash my cheeks. Ease! Ease at last:
She swings to leeward, we can safely run.
Washed over rails our Clare Island dreams,
With storm behind us we straddle the wakeful
Waters that draw us headfast to Inishbofin.

The bows rock as she overtakes the surge.
We neither sleep nor sing nor talk,
But look to the land where the men are mowing.
What will the islanders think of our folly?

The whispering spontaneous reception committee
Nods and smokes by the calm jetty.
Am I jealous of these courteous fishermen
Who hand us ashore, for knowing the sea
Intimately, for respecting the storm

That took nine of their men on one bad night
And five from Rossadillisk in this very boat?
Their harbour is sheltered. They are slow to tell
The story again. There is local pride
In their home-built ships.
We are advised to return next day by the mail.

But tonight we stay, drinking with people
Happy in the monotony of boats,
Bringing the catch to the Cleggan market,
Cultivating fields, or retiring from America
With enough to soak till morning or old age.

The bench below my knees lifts, and the floor
Drops, and the words depart, depart, with faces
Blurred by the smoke. An old man grips my arm,
His shot eyes twitch, quietly dissatisfied.
He has lost his watch, an American gold
From Boston gas-works. He treats the company
To the secretive surge, the sea of his sadness.
I slip outside, fall among stones and nettles,
Crackling dry twigs on an elder tree,
While an accordion drones above the hill.

Later, I reach a room, where the moon stares
Cobwebbed through the window. The tide has ebbed,
Boats are careened in the harbour. Here is a bed.

The Philosopher and the Birds

In memory of Wittgenstein at Rosroe

A solitary invalid in a fuchsia garden
Where time's rain eroded the root since Eden,
He became for a tenebrous epoch the stone.

Here wisdom surrendered the don's gown
Choosing, for Cambridge, two deck chairs,
A kitchen table, undiluted sun.

He clipped with February shears the dead
Metaphysical foliage. Old, in fieldfares
Fantasies rebelled though annihilated.

He was haunted by gulls beyond omega shade,
His nerve tormented by terrified knots
In pin-feathered flesh. But all folly repeats

Is worth one snared robin his fingers untied.
He broke prisons, beginning with words,
And at last tamed, by talking, wild birds.

Through accident of place, now by belief
I follow his love which bird-handled thoughts
To grasp growth's terror or death's leaf.

He last on this savage promontory shored
His logical weapon. Genius stirred
A soaring intolerance to teach a blackbird.

So before alpha you may still hear sing
In the leaf-dark dusk some descended young
Who exalt the evening to a wordless song.

His wisdom widens: he becomes worlds
Where thoughts are wings. But at Rosroe hordes
Of village cats have massacred his birds.

Auction

When furniture is moved
From a dead-free home
Through lean, loved
Rooms alone I come,

To bid for damp etchings,
My great-aunt's chair,
Drawers where rings
Of ruby in water flare.

A sacked gardener
Shows me yew-hedges
House-high, where
The dead made marriages.

With what shall I buy
From time's auctioneers
This old property
Before it disappears?

Girl at the Seaside

To Patricia

I lean on a lighthouse rock
Where the seagowns flow,
A trawler slips from the dock
Sailing years ago.

Wine, tobacco and seamen
Cloud the green air,
A head of snakes in the rain
Talks away desire.

A sailor kisses me
Tasting of mackerel,
I analyse misery
Till mass bells peal.

I wait for clogs on the cobbles,
Dead feet at night,
Only a tempest blows
Darkness on sealight.

I've argued myself here
To the blue cliff-tops:
I'll drop through the sea-air
Till everything stops.

Epitaph on a Fir-tree

She grew ninety years through sombre winter,
Rhododendron summer of midges and rain,
In a beechwood scarred by the auctioneer,

Till a March evening, the garden work done,
It seemed her long life had been completed,
No further growth, no gaiety could remain.

At a wedding breakfast bridesmaids planted
With trowel and gloves this imported fir.
How soon, measured by trees, the party ended.

Arbour and crinoline have gone under
The laurel, gazebos under the yews:
Wood for wood, we have little to compare.

We think no more of granite steps and pews,
Or an officer patched with a crude trepan
Who fought in Rangoon for these quiet acres.

Axes and saws now convert the evergreen
Imperial shadows into deal boards,
And let the sun enter our house again.

Quickly we'll spend the rings that she hoarded
In her gross girth. The evening is ours.
Those delicate girls who earthed her up are faded.

Except for daffodils, the ground is bare:
We two are left. They walked through pergolas
And planted well, so that we might do better.

The Woman of the House

*In memory of my grandmother Lucy Mary Ormsby
whose home was in the west of Ireland
1873–1958*

On a patrician evening in Ireland
I was born in the guest-room: she delivered me.
May I deliver her from the cold hand
Where now she lies, with a brief elegy?

It was her house where we spent holidays,
With candles to bed, and ghostly stories:
In the lake of her heart we were islands
Where the wild asses galloped in the wind.

Her mind was a vague and log-warmed yarn
Spun between sleep and acts of kindliness:
She fed our feelings as dew feeds the grass
On April nights, and our mornings were green:

And those happy days, when in spite of rain
We'd motor west where the salmon-boats tossed,
She would sketch on the pier among the pots
Waves in a sunset, or the rising moon.

Indian-meal porridge and brown soda-bread,
Boiled eggs and buttermilk, honey from gorse,
Far more than we wanted she always offered
In a heart-surfeit: she ate little herself.

Mistress of mossy acres and unpaid rent,
She crossed the walls on foot to feed the sick:
Though frugal cousins frowned on all she spent
People had faith in her healing talent.

She bandaged the wounds that poverty caused
In the house that famine labourers built,
Gave her hands to cure impossible wrong
In a useless way, and was loved for it.

Hers were the fruits of a family tree:
A china clock, the Church's calendar,
Gardeners polite, governesses plenty,
And incomes waiting to be married for.

How the feckless fun would flicker her face
Reading our future by cards at the fire,
Rings and elopements, love-letters, old lace,
A signet of jokes to seal our desire.

"It was sad about Maud, poor Maud!" she'd sigh
To think of the friend she lured and teased
Till she married the butler. "Starved to death,
No service either by padre or priest."

Cholera raged in the Residency:
"They kept my uncle alive on port,"
Which saved him to slaughter a few sepoys
And retire to Galway in search of sport.

The pistol that lost an ancestor's duel,
The hoof of the horse that carried him home
To be stretched on chairs in the drawing-room,
Hung by the Rangoon prints and the Crimean medal.

Lever and Lover, Somerville and Ross
Have fed the same worm as Blackstone and Gibbon,
The mildew has spotted *Clarissa*'s spine
And soiled the *Despatches of Wellington*.

Beside her bed lay an old Bible that
Her Colonel Rector husband used to read,
And a new *Writers' and Artists' Year-book*
To bring a never printed girlhood back.

The undeveloped thoughts died in her head,
But from her heart, through the people she loved
Images spread, and intuitions lived,
More than the mere sense of what she said.

At last, her warmth made ashes of the trees
Ancestors planted, and she was removed
To hospital to die there, certified.
Her house, but not her kindness, has found heirs.

Compulsory comforts penned her limping soul:
With all she uttered they smiled and agreed.
When she summoned the chauffeur, no one obeyed,
But a chrome hearse was ready for nightfall.

"Order the car for nine o'clock tonight!
I must get back, get back. They're expecting me.
I'll bring the spiced beef and the nuts and fruit.
Come home and I'll brew you lime-flower tea!

"The house in flames and nothing is insured!
Send for the doctor, let the horses go.
The dogs are barking again. Has the cow
Calved in the night? What is that great singed bird?

"I don't know who you are, but you've kind eyes.
My children are abroad and I'm alone.
They left me in this gaol. You all tell lies.
You're not my people. My people have gone."

Now she's spent everything: the golden waste
Is washed away, silent her heart's hammer.
The children overseas no longer need her,
They are like aftergrass to her harvest.

People she loved were those who worked the land
Whom the land satisfied more than wisdom:
They've gone, a tractor ploughs where horses strained,
Sometimes sheep occupy their roofless room.

Through our inheritance all things have come,
The form, the means, all by our family:
The good of being alive was given through them,
We ourselves limit that legacy.

The bards in their beds once beat out ballads
Under leaky thatch listening to sea-birds,
But she in the long ascendancy of rain
Served biscuits on a tray with ginger wine.

Time can never relax like this again,
She in her phaeton looking for folk-lore,
He writing sermons in the library
Till lunch, then fishing all the afternoon.

On a wet winter evening in Ireland
I let go her hand, and we buried her
In the family earth beside her husband.
Only to think of her, now warms my mind.

Years Later

From *The Cleggan Disaster*

Whose is that hulk on the shingle
The boatwright's son repairs
Though she has not been fishing
For thirty-four years
Since she rode the disaster?
The oars were turned into rafters
For a roof stripped by a gale.
Moss has grown on her keel.

Where are the red-haired women
Chattering along the piers
Who gutted millions of mackerel
And baited the spillet hooks
With mussels and lug-worms?
All the hurtful hours
Thinking the boats were coming
They hold against those years.

Where are the barefoot children
With brown toes in the ashes
Who went to the well for water,
Picked winkles on the beach
And gathered sea-rods in winter?
The lime is green on the stone
Which they once kept white-washed.
In summer nettles return.

Where are the dances in houses
With porter and cakes in the room,
The reddled faces of fiddlers
Sawing out jigs and reels,

The flickering eyes of neighbours?
The thatch which was neatly bordered
By a fringe of sea-stones
Has now caved in.

Why does she stand at the curtains
Combing her seal-grey hair
And uttering bitter opinions
On land-work and sea-fear,
Drownings and famines?
When will her son say,
"Forget about the disaster,
We're mounting nets today!"

From The Last Galway Hooker

I chose to renew her, to rebuild, to prolong
For a while the spliced yards of yesterday.
Carpenters were enrolled, the ballast and the dung

Of cattle she'd carried lifted from the hold,
The engine removed, and the stale bilge scoured.
De Valera's daughter hoisted the Irish flag

At her freshly adzed mast this Shrove Tuesday,
Stepped while afloat between the tackle of the *Topaz*
And the *St. John*, by Bofin's best boatsmen,

All old as herself. Her skilful sailmaker,
Her inherited boatwright, her dream-tacking steersman
Picked up the tools of their interrupted work,

And in memory's hands this hooker was restored.
Old men my instructors, and with all new gear
May I handle her well down tomorrow's sea-road.

The Poet on the Island

To Theodore Roethke

On a wet night, laden with books for luggage,
And stumbling under the burden of himself,
He reached the pier, looking for a refuge.

Darkly he crossed to the island six miles off:
The engine pulsed, the sails invented rhythm,
While the sea expanded and the rain drummed softly.

Safety on water, he rocked with a new theme:
And in the warmth of his mind's greenhouse bloomed
A poem nurtured like a chrysanthemum.

His forehead, a Prussian helmet, moody, domed,
Relaxed in the sun: a lyric was his lance.
To be loved by the people, he, a stranger, hummed

In the herring-store on Sunday crammed with drunks
Ballads of bawdry with a speakeasy stress.
Yet lonely they left him, "one of the Yanks."

The children understood. This was not madness.
How many orphans had he fathered in words
Robust and cunning, but never heartless.

He watched the harbour scouted by sea-birds:
His fate was like fish under poetry's beaks:
Words began weirdly to take off inwards.

Time that they calendar in seasons not in clocks,
In gardens dug over and houses roofed,
Was to him a see-saw of joys and shocks,

Where his body withered but his style improved.
A storm shot up, his glass cracked in a gale:
An abstract thunder of darkness deafened

The listeners he'd once given roses, now hail.
He'd burst the lyric barrier: logic ended.
Doctors were called, and he agreed to sail.

Aughrim

Who owns the land where musket-balls are buried
In blackthorn roots on the eskar, the drained bogs
Where sheep browse, and credal war miscarried?
Names in the rival churches are written on plaques.

Behind the dog-rose ditch, defended with pikes,
A tractor sprays a rood of flowering potatoes:
Morning fog is lifting, and summer hikers
Bathe in a stream passed by cavalry traitors.

A Celtic cross by the road commemorates no battle
But someone killed in a car, Minister of Agriculture.
Dairy lorries on the fast trunk-route rattle:
A girl cycles along the lane to meet her lover.

Flies gyrate in their galaxy above my horse's head
As he ambles and shies close to the National School—
Bullets under glass, Patrick Sarsfield's *Would to God . . .*—
And jolts me bareback on the road for Battle Hill:

Where a farmer with a tinker woman hired to stoop
Is thinning turnips by hand, while giant earth-movers
Shovel and claw a highway over the rector's glebe:
Starlings worm the aftergrass, a barley crop silvers,

And a rook tied by the leg to scare flocks of birds
Croaks as I dismount at the death-cairn of St. Ruth:
Le jour est à nous, mes enfants, his last words:
A cannonball beheaded him, and sowed a myth.

History

One morning of arrested growth
An army list roll-called the sound
Of perished names, but I found no breath
In dog-eared inventories of death.

Touch unearths military history.
Sifting clay on a mound, I find
Bones and bullets fingering my mind:
The past is happening today.

The battle cause, a handgrenade
Lobbed in a playground, the king's viciousness
With slaves succumbing to his rod and kiss,
Has a beginning in my blood.

Rapparees

Out of the earth, out of the air, out of the water
And slinking nearer the fire, in groups they gather:
Once he looked like a bird, but now a beggar.

This fish rainbows out of a pool: "Give me bread!"
He fins along the lake-shore with the starved.
Green eyes glow in the night from clumps of weed.

The water is still. A rock or the nose of an otter
Jars the surface. Whistle of rushes or bird?
It steers to the bank, it lands as a pikeman armed.

With flint and bundles of straw a limestone hall
Is gutted, a noble family charred in its sleep,
And they gloat by moonlight on a mound of rubble.

The highway trees are gibbets where seventeen rot
Who were caught last week in a cattle-raid.
The beasts are lowing. "Listen!" "Stifle the guard!"

In a pinewood thickness an earthed-over charcoal fire
Forges them guns. They melt lead stripped from a steeple
For ball. At the whirr of a snipe each can disappear

Terrified as a bird in a gorse-bush fire,
To delve like a mole or mingle like a nightjar
Into the earth, into the air, into the water.

Planter

Seven candles in silver sticks,
Water on an oval table,
The painted warts of Cromwell
Framed in a sullen gold.
There was ice on the axe
When it hacked the king's head.
Moths drown in the dripping wax.

Slow sigh of the garden yews
Forty years planted.
May the God of battle
Give us this day our land
And the papists be trampled.
Softly my daughter plays
Sefauchi's Farewell.

Dark night with no moon to guard
Roads from the rapparees,
Food at a famine price,
Cattle raided, corn trod,
And the servants against us
With our own guns and swords.
Stress a hymn to peace.

Quiet music and claret cups,
Forty acres of green crops
Keep far from battle
My guest, with a thousand troops
Following his clan-call,
Red-mouthed O'Donnell.
I bought him: the traitor sleeps.

To whom will the land belong
This time tomorrow night?
I am loyal to fields I have sown
And the king reason elected:
Not to a wine-blotted birth-mark
Of prophecy, but hard work
Deepening the soil for seed.

Wolfhound

A wolfhound sits under a wild ash
Licking the wound in a dead ensign's neck.

When guns cool at night with bugles in fog
She points over the young face.

All her life a boy's pet.
Prisoners are sabred and the dead are stripped.

Her ear pricks like a crimson leaf on snow,
The horse-carts creak away.

Vermin by moonlight pick
The tongues and sockets of six thousand skulls.

She pines for his horn to blow
To bay in triumph down the track of wolves.

Her forelegs stand like pillars through a siege,
His Toledo sword corrodes.

Nights she lopes to the scrub
And trails back at dawn to guard a skeleton.

Wind shears the berries from the rowan tree,
The wild geese have flown.

She lifts her head to cry
As a woman keens in a famine for her son.

A redcoat, stalking, cocks
His flintlock when he hears the wolfhound growl.

Her fur bristles with fear at the new smell,
Snow has betrayed her lair.

"I'll sell you for a packhorse,
You antiquated bigoted papistical bitch!"

She springs: in self-defence he fires his gun.
People remember this.

By turf embers she gives tongue
When the choirs are silenced in wood and stone.

Luttrell's Death

Luttrell, Master of Luttrellstown
Sat in a gold and red sedan
The burden of a hungry urchin
And a weak old man
Barefoot on cobbles in the midnight rain,
Up torchlit quays from a coffee shop
Where after supper, the silver cup
Lifted, a fop had said
"It's time to bury Aughrim's dead."

A poor smell of ordure
Seeped through his embroidered chair,
He slid the glass open for air,
Waved off a beggar groping at the door
And watched six black dray-horses cross
The river. "Let the traitor pass."
He felt his pocket full of pebbles
Which he used at Mass in straw-roofed chapels
To lob at little girls.

The chair slewed at his town house,
Flambeaus, footmen in place,
And plunked him down.
He'd sold his country to preserve his class,
The gutters hissed: but that was done
Twenty-six years ago, he said,
Had they not buried Aughrim's dead?
Standing under grey cut stone
A shadow cocked a gun.

No one betrayed his assassin
Although the Duke of Bolton
Offered three hundred pounds' reward.
The crowd spat on Henry Luttrell's coffin.
Eighty years after his murder
Masked men, inspired by Wolfe Tone,
Burst open his tomb's locks,
Lit a stub of wax
And smashed the skull with a pickaxe.

Patrick Sarsfield

Sarsfield, great-uncle in the portrait's grime,
Your emigration built your fame at home.
Landlord who never racked, you gave your rent
To travel with your mounted regiment.

Hotly you duelled for our name abroad
In Restoration wig, with German sword,
Wanting a vicious murder thrust to prove
Your Celtic passion and our Lady's love.

Gallant at Sedgemoor, cutting down for James
The scythe-armed yokels Monmouth led like lambs,
You thought it needed God's anointed king
To breathe our Irish winter into spring.

Your ashwood lance covered the Boyne retreat:
When the divine perfidious monarch's rout
From kindred enemy and alien friend
Darkened the land, you kindled Ireland.

At Limerick besieged, you led the dance:
"If this had failed, I would have gone to France."
When youths lit brandy in a pewter dish
You were their hazel nut and speckled fish.

A French duke scoffed: "They need no cannonballs
But roasted apples to assault these walls."
Sarsfield, through plague and shelling you held out;
You saved the city, lost your own estate.

Shunning pitched battle was your strategy:
You chose rapparee mountain routes to try
The enemy's morale, and blew his train
Of cannon skywards in the soft night rain.

Your king, who gave St. Ruth supreme command,
Mistrusted you, native of Ireland.
"Await further orders," you were told
At Aughrim, when your plan was overruled.

You stood, while brother officers betrayed
By going, and six thousand Irish died.
Then you assumed command, but veered about:
Chose exile in your courteous conqueror's boat.

"Change kings with us, and we will fight again,"
You said, but sailed off with ten thousand men;
While women clutched the hawsers in your wake,
Drowning—it was too late when you looked back.

Only to come home stronger had you sailed:
Successes held you, and the French prevailed.
Coolly you triumphed where you wanted least,
On Flemish cornfield or at Versailles feast.

We loved you, horseman of the white cockade,
Above all, for your last words, "Would to God
This wound had been for Ireland." Cavalier,
You feathered with the wild geese our despair.

From The God who Eats Corn

To my Father

Tall in his garden, shaded and brick-walled,
He upholds the manners of a lost empire.
Time has confused dead honour with dead guilt
But lets a sunbird sip at a gold creeper.

His scholar's head, disguised in a bush hat,
Spectacled eyes, that watch the weaver's nest
Woven, have helped a high dam to be built
Where once the Zambesi was worshipped and wasted.

Sometimes he dreams of a rogue elephant
That smashed the discharged rifle in his hand:
Or reading, remembers the horns of buffalo,
The leopards he shipped to the Dublin zoo.

At dusk on the stoep he greets ambassadors
From Kenya and Ceylon. The silver trays
Are lit by candles cupped in the flower borders.
Husks hang on his dry indaba trees.

Last thing at night he checks the rain-gauge
Remembering his father on a rectory lawn.
Thunder is pent in the drums of the compound.
He feels too old to love the rising moon.

Little Hunger

I drove to Little Hunger promontory
   Looking for pink stone
In roofless houses huddled by the sea
   To buy to build my own.

Hovels to live in, ruins to admire
   From a car cruising by,
The weathered face caught in a sunset fire,
   Hollowed with exility;

Whose gradual fall my purchase would complete,
   Clearing them off the land,
The seven cabins needed to create
   The granite house I planned.

Once mine, I'd work on their dismemberment,
   Threshold, lintel, wall;
And pick a hearthstone from a rubble fragment
   To make it integral.

Lullaby

Before you'd given death a name
Like bear or crocodile, death came

To take your mother out one night.
But when she'd said her last good night

You cried, "I don't want you to go,"
So in her arms she took you too.

Mary Ure

Bare feet she dips across my boat's blue rail
In the ocean as we run under full white summer sail.
The cold spray kisses them. She's not immortal.

Sitting in her orchard she reads *Lady Lazarus*
Aloud rehearsing, when her smallest child lays
Red peonies in her lap with tender apologies.

She walks by Lough Mask in a blue silk gown
So thin the cloudy wind is biting to the bone
But she talks as lightly as if the sun shone.

Walking on Sunday

Walking on Sunday into Omey Island
　　When the tide had fallen slack,
I crossed a spit of wet ribbed sand
　　With a cold breeze at my back.

Two sheepdogs nosed me at a stile,
　　Boys chevied on the green,
A woman came out of a house to smile
　　And tell me she had seen

Men digging down at St. Fechin's church,
　　Buried in sand for centuries
Up to its pink stone gable top, a perch
　　For choughs and seapies.

I found a dimple scalloped from a dune,
　　A landing-slip for coracles,
Two graveyards—one for women, one for men—
　　Odorous of miracles:

And twelve parishioners probing a soft floor
　　To find what solid shape there was
Under shell-drift; seeking window, door;
　　And measuring the house.

Blood was returning dimly to the face
　　Of the chancel they'd uncovered,
Granite skin that rain would kiss
　　Until the body flowered.

41

I heard the spades clang with a shock
  Inaugurating spring:
Fechin used plug and feather to split rock
  And poised the stone to sing.

He tuned cacophony to make
  Harmony in this choir:
The ocean gorged on it, he died of plague,
  And hawks nested there.

Coppersmith

A temple tree grew in our garden in Ceylon.
We knew it by no other name.
The flower, if you turned it upside down,
Looked like a dagoba with an onion dome.
A holy perfume
Stronger than the evil tang of betel-nut
Enticed me into its shade on the stuffiest afternoon,

Where I stood and listened to the tiny hammer-stroke
Of the crimson coppersmith perched above my head,
His *took took took*
And his *tonk tonk tonk*
Were spoken in a language I never understood:
And there I began to repeat
Out loud to myself an English word such as *beat beat beat*,

Till hammering too hard I lost the meaning in the sound
Which faded and left nothing behind,
A blank mind,
The compound spinning round,
My brain melting, as if I'd stood in the sun
Too long without a topee and was going blind,
Till I and the bird, the word and the tree, were one.

Firebug

He's tired of winding up the gramophone
Half way through "Three Little Maids",
And waiting for a rickshaw to return from the bazaar.
The monsoon teems on the compound.
A coolie, splitting coconuts on an iron spike,
Stoops to wring the rain out of his loin-cloth.
The boy picks up a box of matches.

His little sister comes from the nursery holding a doll.
"Give me that!" "What for?"
"I want to set it on fire." "You wouldn't dare."
"I will if you help me."
She puts the doll on the floor. He strikes a match
And holds it gingerly under the pink legs.
The girl screeches like a cockatoo.

The fire bursts into song,
Eats the doll, sticks out its tongue, stands up
Gyrating like a crimson top: then dies.
Burnt celluloid leaves a guilty smell.
The girl cries over the ashes, "Give me back my doll!"
"An angel took it to heaven, didn't you see?"
The devil needs thrashing with a shoe.

Traveller's Palm

You take off your new blancoed shoes at the temple door.
She wraps them in tissue paper,
Humming her favourite bar of *Pomp and Circumstance.*
Lightly your feet slip, feeling the cool marble floor.
"Stop showing off! Remember where you are!"
Flambeaux, tom-toms, flageolets, incense.
Devil-dancers, with a clash of cymbals, begin to dance.

They hobble and sway above you on bamboo stilts:
Crocodile, panther, jackal, monkey, toad:
Tongues hanging out, paddy-straw hair, boils and welts
On bums with tails, torsos gummy as rubber trees,
Jungle-fowl feathers glued on thighs.
Each bears the spots or sores of an incurable disease.
Copper bells clang on elbows, ankles and knees.

They block the corridor you've got to pass. Their sweat
Steams like monsoon rain on a path of dust.
Coconut cressets, carried by almost naked men,
Burn with a sickening fume.
"Nan, I'm thirsty. Can't we go home?"
Your mouth is as dry as pith on a mango stone.
You turn and bury your head in her old green gown.

She smarms your hair, tightens the knot in your silk tie:
Takes you out on a high cool balcony
Freed from the ant-hill crowd.
Huge howdahed elephants lumber out of a wood,
Trapped under jewelled caparisons. Gongs and floodlight.
"When I grow up, will you let me marry you?"
"By the time you're old enough, I'll be buried in Timbuktu."

A monk hangs a garland of temple flowers round your neck.
Tea-planters chatter and smoke.
"How did the Tooth fit in Buddha's mouth?"
"It must be a tiger's. Nobody knows the truth."
Can't you see which elephant carries the holy relic?
Pain jabs your heart. Poison! You almost cry.
Doesn't she realize? Won't she believe? You're going to die.

A pigeon's blood ruby sparkles in Lady Weerasirie's nose.
Hum of malarial mosquitoes.
Worse and worse the pain. "Can we go home soon?"
At the temple door you put on your shoes.
A tonsured priest in a saffron robe is bowing. "Goodbye."
Mind you don't step on a scorpion.
Full moon, tree-frogs, fire-flies: a brutal jungle cry.

Your throat's burning. Will there be time to reach home
And call Dr. Chisel? Look, here's a traveller's palm.
She shows you the place to sink
The point of the ivory pen-knife you won in a race:
A dark olive leaf-sheath curving out of a dry old stem.
If you die, can you be reborn? Try!
Even if the water of the tree is poison, drink!

Jurors

—Why did he kill her? Jealousy, anger, drink?
There's always more to it than what you hear.

—It had to happen, it was coming to her,
Unfortunate girl, since the day she was born.
He used to work as a turfcutter:
The man she left him for drove a van in town.

—Why are they taking so long to arrest
If they saw him follow her out of the hall,
And found her shoe on the road, her body pressed
Head first into a stream behind a wall?

—They've sent away his boots to be analysed,
And a few ribs they found of her chestnut hair.

Double Negative

To Tony White

You were standing on the quay
Wondering who was the stranger on the mailboat
While I was on the mailboat
Wondering who was the stranger on the quay

Pat Cloherty's Version of
The Maisie

I've no tooth to sing you the song
   Tierney made at the time
     but I'll tell the truth

It happened on St. John's Day
   sixty-eight years ago
     last June the twenty-fourth

The Maisie sailed from Westport Quay
   homeward on a Sunday
     missing Mass to catch the tide

John Kerrigan sat at her helm
   Michael Barrett stood at her mast
     and Kerrigan's wife lay down below

The men were two stepbrothers
   drownings in the family
     and all through the family

Barrett kept a shop in the island
   Kerrigan plied the hooker
     now deeply laden with flour

She passed Clare and she came to Cahir
   two reefs tied in the mainsail
     she bore a foresail but no jib

South-east wind with strong ebb-tide
   still she rode   this way   that way
      hugging it   hugging it   O my dear

And it blew and blew hard and blew hard
   but Kerrigan kept her to it
      as long as he was there he kept her to it

Rain fell in a cloudburst
   hailstones hit her deck
      there was no return for him once he'd put out

At Inishturk when the people saw
   The Maisie smothered up in darkness
      they lit candles in the church

What more could Kerrigan do?
   he put her jaw into the hurricane
      and the sea claimed him

Barrett was not a sailor
   to take a man from the water
      the sea claimed him too

At noon the storm ceased
   and we heard *The Maisie*'d foundered
      high upon a Mayo strand

The woman came up from the forecastle
   she came up alone on deck
      and a great heave cast her out on shore

And another heave came while she drowned
   and put her on her knees
      like a person'd be in prayer

That's the way the people found her
　and the sea never came in
　　near that mark no more

John Kerrigan was found
　far down at Achill Sound
　　he's buried there

Michael Barrett was taken
　off Murrisk Pier
　　he's buried there

Kerrigan's wife was brought from Cross
　home to Inishbofin
　　and she's buried there

Song for a Corncrake

Why weave rhetoric on your voice's loom,
Shuttling at the bottom of my garden
In meadowsweet and broom?
Crepuscular, archaic politician,
It's time to duck down,
Little bridegroom.

Why draft an epic on a myth of doom
In staunchly nailed iambics
Launched nightly near my room?
Since all you need to say is *crex*
Give us lyrics,
Little bridegroom.

Why go on chiselling mottoes for a tomb,
Counting on a scythe to spare
Your small defenceless home?
Quicken your tune, O improvise, before
The combine and the digger come,
Little bridegroom.

The Reading Lesson

Fourteen years old, learning the alphabet,
He finds letters harder to catch than hares
Without a greyhound. Can't I give him a dog
To track them down, or put them in a cage?
He's caught in a trap, until I let him go,
Pinioned by "Don't you want to learn to read?"
"I'll be the same man whatever I do."

He looks at a page as a mule balks at a gap
From which a goat may hobble out and bleat.
His eyes jink from a sentence like flushed snipe
Escaping shot. A sharp word, and he'll mooch
Back to his piebald mare and bantam cock.
Our purpose is as tricky to retrieve
As mercury from a smashed thermometer.

"I'll not read any more." Should I give up?
His hands, long-fingered as a Celtic scribe's,
Will grow callous, gathering sticks or scrap;
Exploring pockets of the horny drunk
Loiterers at the fairs, giving them lice.
A neighbour chuckles. "You can never tame
The wild-duck: when his wings grow, he'll fly off."

If books resembled roads, he'd quickly read:
But they're small farms to him, fenced by the page,
Ploughed into lines, with letters drilled like oats:
A field of tasks he'll always be outside.
If words were bank-notes, he would filch a wad;
If they were pheasants, they'd be in his pot
For breakfast, or if wrens he'd make them king.

Care

Kidded in April above Glencolumbkille
On a treeless hill backing north, she throve
Sucking milk off heather and rock, until

I came with children to buy her. We drove
South, passing Drumcliff. Restless in the car,
Bleating, she gulped at plastic teats we'd shove

Copiously in her mouth. Soon she'd devour
Whatever we'd give. Prettily she poked
Her gypsy head with hornbuds through barbed wire

To nip off pea-tops, her fawn pelt streaked
With Black Forest shadow and Alpine snow.
I stalled her wildness in a pen that locked.

She grew tame and fat, fed on herbs I knew
Her body needed. We ransacked Kylemore
To bring her oakleaf, ivy and bark to chew.

I gutted goatbooks, learning how to cure
Fluke, pulpy kidney, black garget, louping ill:
All my attention bled to cope with her.

No fenceless commonage to roam, no hill
Transfigured into cloud, no dragon wood
To forage with a puck-led flock: but the rattle

Of a bucket, shouts of children bringing food
Across a frozen yard. Out in a forest
She would have known a bad leaf from a good.

Here, captive to our taste, she'd learnt to trust
The petting hand with crushed oats, or a new
Mash of concentrates, or sweet bits of waste.

So when a child mistook a sprig of yew
And mixed it with her fodder, she descried
No danger: we had tamed her instinct too.

Whiskey, white of egg, linseed oil, we tried
Forcing down antidotes. Nothing would do.
The children came to tell me when she died.

Shelter

To Ann

Girl with a sheaf of rye-straw in your arms
How much you carry from a loaded trailer
Parked at the door in a stray sunny shaft
At the tail end of summer, deep into the barn
To store for thatch, if ever we get the weather
Or the time, before winter sets in, how much
You help me, child, in the hour after school,
Hour of your release, face wet with tears
That well up out of a cruelty done to you,
Bruise-marks around your lips, a speechless harm,
How much you help me to make the dark inside
Glitter with sheaves bound firm to keep out storm.
Hear how they rustle as we lay them down:
Their broken heads are thrashed clean of grain.

Granite Globe

Straining my back
Seven times I've lifted you
Up to my thighs

There are men
Who've put you sitting
High on their shoulders

It looks as if you'd been
Lopped
Off the top of a column

Then used as a quern
Kicked around
Buried

An archaeologist
Taped you
And wrote you down

He said
You're an oblate spheroid
Does it matter?

Whoever carved you
Gave you all
The time in the world

High Island

A shoulder of rock
Sticks high up out of the sea,
A fisherman's mark
For lobster and blue-shark.

Fissile and stark
The crust is flaking off,
Seal-rock, gull-rock,
Cove and cliff.

Dark mounds of mica schist,
A lake, mill and chapel,
Roofless, one gable smashed,
Lie ringed with rubble.

An older calm,
The kiss of rock and grass,
Pink thrift and white sea-campion,
Flowers in the dead place.

Day keeps lit a flare
Round the north pole all night
Like brushing long wavy hair
Petrels quiver in flight.

Quietly as the rustle
Of an arm entering a sleeve,
They slip down to nest
Under altar-stone or grave.

Round the wrecked laura
Needles flicker
Tacking air, quicker and quicker
To rock, sea and star.

Stormpetrel

Gipsy of the sea
In winter wambling over scurvy whaleroads,
Jooking in the wake of ships,
A sailor hooks you
And carves his girl's name on your beak.

Guest of the storm
Who sweeps you off to party after party,
You flit in a sooty grey coat
Smelling of must
Barefoot across a sea of broken glass.

Waif of the afterglow
On summer nights to meet your mate you jink
Over sea-cliff and graveyard,
Creeping underground
To hatch an egg in a hermit's skull.

Pulse of the rock
You throb till daybreak on your cryptic nest
A song older than fossils,
Ephemeral as thrift.
It ends with a gasp.

Nocturne

The blade of a knife
Is tapped gently on an oak table
Waves are sobbing in coves

Light bleeds on the sky's rim
From dusk till dawn
Petrels fly in from the ocean

Wings beating on stone
Quick vibration of notes throats tongues
Under silverweed   calling and calling

Louder cries cut the air
They rise from a pit
Complaints are retched up and lost

A solo tune
Is dying with passion
For someone out there to come quickly

Come back   come back
I'm here   here   here
This burrow   this wall   this hole

Ach   who kept you?   where've you been?
There   there   there
It's all over   over   over

Seals at High Island

To Emily

The calamity of seals begins with jaws.
Born in caverns that reverberate
With endless malice of the sea's tongue
Clacking on shingle, they learn to bark back
In fear and sadness and celebration.
The ocean's mouth opens forty feet wide
And closes on a morsel of their rock.

Swayed by the thrust and backfall of the tide,
A dappled grey bull and a brindled cow
Copulate in the green water of a cove.
I watch from a cliff-top, trying not to move.
Sometimes they sink and merge into black shoals;
Then rise for air, his muzzle on her neck,
Their winged feet intertwined as a fishtail.

She opens her fierce mouth like a scarlet flower
Full of white seeds; she holds it open long
At the sunburst in the music of their loving;
And cries a little. But I must remember
How far their feelings are from mine marooned.
If there are tears at this holy ceremony
Theirs are caused by brine and mine by breeze.

When the great bull withdraws his rod, it glows
Like a carnelian candle set in jade.
The cow ripples ashore to feed her calf;
While an old rival, eyeing the deed with hate,
Swims to attack the tired triumphant god.
They rear their heads above the boiling surf,
Their terrible jaws open, jetting blood.

At nightfall they haul out, and mourn the drowned,
Playing to the sea sadly their last quartet,
An improvised requiem that ravishes
Reason, while ripping scale up like a net:
Brings pity trembling down the rocky spine
Of headlands, till the bitter ocean's tongue
Swells in their cove, and smothers their sweet song.